ALOHA KĀUA

WEST MAUI BOOK SERIES

Series Editor:
Lance D. Collins

The West Maui Book Series, written by local scholars and community leaders, explores and documents the history, culture, and social change of and in West Maui.

Proceedings of the Charter Commissions of the County of Maui
Public Access to the Roads and Trails of West Maui
Keka'a: The Making and Saving of North Beach West Maui
The Storied Places of West Maui
Tourism Impacts West Maui
Social Change in West Maui
The Journal of James Macrae: Botanist at the Sandwich Islands, 1825
Lei Nāhonoapi'ilani: Songs of West Maui
Malu 'Ulu o Lele: Maui Komohana in Ka Nupepa Kuokoa
Civil Society in West Maui
Index to the Lahaina News, *the* Lahaina Sun, *and the* Lahaina Times
Water and Power in West Maui
Thinking about Traffic in West Maui
'Ohu'ohu nā Mauna o 'E'eka: Place Names of Maui Komohana
Whose Future?: Community Planning in West Maui
Historical Investigations in West Maui
Reference Guide to the Archaeology of West Maui
Remembering Lahaina
Aloha Kāua

ALOHA KĀUA

NOALANI HELELĀ

Lahaina, Maui, Hawaiʻi

Printed in the United States of America

First printing, 2026

ISBN 978-1-9524-6113-2 (pbk : alk. paper)

Published by the North Beach-West Maui Benefit Fund, Inc.
P O Box 11329
Lahaina, Hawai'i 96761

Distributed by University of Hawai'i Press
2840 Kolowalu Street
Honolulu, HI 96822-1888

This book is printed on acid-free paper and
meets the guidelines for permanence and durability
of the Council on Library Resources.

Print-ready files provided by North Beach-West Maui Benefit Fund, Inc.

Contents

Foreword

There is something about great fiction that reveals the truth of a situation or person more profoundly—capturing the essence, or spirit, instead of the proverbial letter or mere biology. Generations of artists reacting against Realism believed in the same notion: that what we see with our eyes is not real. There is an inner truth, and that invisible yet indelible truth is beautiful. As Khaled Hosseini said, "Writing fiction is the act of weaving a series of lies to arrive at an even greater truth."

In Noalani Helelā's exquisite work of drama, we have told several lies to honor the truth that she is seeking to show. For example, Boki was (presumably) dead by the time any of this story unfolds, the use of throne/palace/crown are metaphorical (indeed, there was a diarchy not a monarchy), the royal guard (described by Iʻi in his story about Kīnaʻū's marriage to Kekūanaōʻa) appears differently, each aliʻi would have been surrounded by attendants—never moving alone as they are on our limited stage (O for a muse of fire...), Queen Kaʻahumanu famously wore yellow (or stripes), Kauikeaouli built a wall not a fence, and aliʻi enjoyed but did not dance hula (someone of Liliha's status certainly would not have).

Of course no one bats an eyelash when Shakespeare has Percy and Hal fighting each other in single combat, or Richard crying out on the battlefield "my kingdom for a horse!" But perhaps that's because so many Western stories are told—there is less urgency, no danger—how can there be any peril when there are so many of them? The problem is, when brilliant indigenous playwrights like Helelā are chastised for making important dramatic choices that serve the story and the truth, it discourages future playwrights.

There should be a dialogue; there needs to be feedback—but there also needs to be radical inclusion, and an understanding of the sovereignty of any artist in the construction of her narrative. Kaomi was nearly erased from history—so few sources even mention him. It is a sad story.

But drama must respond to the needs of society. We are so inundated with escapist entertainment and feel-good fairytales—what a society needs is not always what it wants. Drama must remind us that we can be the heroes of our own narratives, that other tragic stories have happened, and we have survived those too, and others have stood up, and we will stand on their backs, and see even further into the horizon.

Ultimately, the truth of Helelā's historic drama is love. Love transforms, ignites, nurtures, and inspires. Almost two hundred years ago, two young men fell in love. Instead of giving up love, the king sentenced himself to hard labor; instead of giving up love, Kaomi faced physical violence; instead of giving up love, they stood before an entire kingdom and embraced, and scorned the bigots whose eyes were too blinded by shallow, corporeal lies, too focused on fear to ever hope for the future. ("God is love, and whoever loves knows God" John 4:16.)

Helelā's play is the somewhat fictive and yet totally truthful story of two men who change because of each other and together face a changing world. As Albert Camus wrote, "Fiction is the lie through which we tell the truth."

Taurie Kinoshita
Director of the World Premiere

Preface

With historical fiction, inaccuracies are inevitable, and luckily, our brilliant director Taurie Kinoshita and amazing cast helped to mitigate that as much as possible and give life to this show that I struggled to write.

I've never written historical fiction before, let alone retold an often untold part of history that involves possibly the first known case of anti-queer violence to happen in Hawai'i.

While I'm grateful to have been given the opportunity, many points of the writing process were extremely painful and took a lot out of me, especially as a queer Hawaiian woman who loves my partner more than words could describe (who, by the way, I would not have been able to write this show without). I put a lot of pressure on myself to portray the people and events respectfully, and not to anger the ancestors and community. While there was only so much I could do, I hope that pressure paid off.

Noalani Helelā

Aloha Kāua *premiered at*
Palikū Theatre, Oʻahu, Hawaiʻi
February 21–March 2, 2025
and
ʻĪao Theater, Maui, Hawaiʻi
March 8–March 9, 2025

ALOHA KĀUA

Cast of Characters

KAUIKEAOULI	Young monarch navigating leadership, legacy, and personal conviction
KAOMI	Hawaiian/Tahitian preacher and healer, torn between faith and identity
KAʻAHUMANU	Queen Regent devoted to Christian reform and national preservation
KĪNAʻU	Sister of Kauikeaouli: principled, poised, and politically astute
HIRAM BINGHAM	Missionary advisor advocating Christian authority and order
KEKŪANAŌʻA	Traditionalist chief upholding royal lineage and cultural norms
BOKI	Former governor: worldly, wise, and Kaomi's spiritual guide
LILIHA	Governor of Oʻahu, fiercely intelligent and culturally resolute
KAIKIOʻEWA	Governor of Kauaʻi, vocal critic of royal and religious decisions
KAIHUHANUNA	Lesser chief: present in court, loyal to aliʻi leadership
KAPILI	Earnest royal attendant: fervently loyal and theatrically devoted
KIMO and ZIMO	Palace guards or attendants with minimal but steady presence
KALEO and KŪLANI	Distillery workers: playful with dice and drink, yet humble and deferential before authority
MAN	Commoner, seeks Kaomi's judgment in a land dispute, humble yet resilient

Time and Place

Set in the Hawaiian Kingdom of the early nineteenth century, the play moves between Lahaina, Maui and Oʻahu, unfolding in royal and political settings during a period of profound cultural and political change.

ACT ONE

SCENE 1

Various formally dressed people, many of them Hawaiian, sit together in the pews of a church in Lahaina with light peering through the stained glass, as KAOMI*, a half-Tahitian, half Hawaiian man dressed in traditional priest's clothing, delivers a sermon to the Calvinist congregation.*

KAOMI

'Tis these times during which we must remember, that much akin to the sails of a wa'a, healing is a process that seldom charges straightforwardly. With an ebb and flow in which we must learn to rock and sway does it move. And amidst this perilous voyage, 'tis upon our Great Almighty God, Ke Akua, and our halo-lorn ancestors at his sides, to illuminate the onward seas as they have thus far. Fear not the flame-like waves in their attempts to engulf our ship in a drowning blaze. Fear not the rumbling clouds, darkening like sins carried from our cradles. Fear not the transformation of our femurs to brackish water leaking from our uncertain hearts, and instead, how to stand upon them once again we must learn.

Almighty and eternal God, we desire to praise thy holy name, for so graciously raising us up, in soundness of body and mind, to see the light of this day. We bless thee on behalf of all thy creatures, for "the eyes of all look unto thee, and you give them their meat in due season." But above all we acknowledge thine inestimable benefits bestowed upon mankind in Christ Jesus. We thank thee for his miraculous birth, his most holy life, his bitter agony, his bloody death, his glorious resurrection on this day, his ascension into heaven, his triumph over all the powers of darkness, and his sitting at thy right hand for evermore. Amen.

(As the service ends, people file out of church and HIRAM BINGHAM *strolls over to* KAOMI*, shaking his hand.)*

HIRAM

Inspired speech, Reverend Kaomi.

KAOMI

Thank you, Royal Advisor Bingham.

Dare I with utmost reverence ask of Your Majesty's business here?! Quite aware you are that you must be present alongside the royal guard, are you not?

KAUIKEAOULI

Am I now prohibited visitation of this sacred house of worship during a desperate demand of spiritual guidance?

KAOMI

Has it crossed Your Majesty's vastly open mind that perhaps demand would be less desperate, were rebellion of minor appeal to you?

KAUIKEAOULI

Existence was my foremost act of rebellion. I find great appeal in that.

KAOMI

If I may be so brazen, it appears you find even greater appeal in a flare for the dramatic.

KAUIKEAOULI

None but a true friend would take note of that.

KAOMI

Lest you forget, you are no friend of mine, but a king of the people.

KAUIKEAOULI

And your words are a force for healing the masses, not for the stinging of my na'au.

KAOMI

Alas, the aforementioned flare can be seen once again.

(Royal servant KAPILI *suddenly runs in, completely out of breath.)*

KAPILI

Your Majesty . . . I was sent . . . by Queen Regent Ka'ahumanu . . . to fetch you . . . but first you must pardon me for a moment . . . I believe that at the palace . . . I may have left . . . my lungs. . . .

KAUIKEAOULI

Oh Kapili . . . such a dutiful subject you are, but little urgency do I see in returning this instant. My magnificently powerful mother shall ensure some method of survival. Much faith I have in her.

KAOMI

With humility, how someone may be so filled with elegance and frivolous rebellion at once remains beyond my comprehension. . . .

KAUIKEAOULI

I seem to recall some accounts of our ancestors emphasizing the importance of dualities. . . .

KAOMI

Doth that provide explanation on how you may banter idly with a common half-caste priest—

KAUIKEAOULI

I firmly disagree that your Tahitian ancestry is warranting of such nomenclature—

KAOMI

—whilst providing a chiefly address opposite this side of town?

KAUIKEAOULI

Oh Lord, my address!

(KAPILI finally catching his breath.)

KAPILI

Yes, Your Majesty, that is what I have been attempting to alert you of.

(KAOMI reaches under his priest's clothing and pulls out a chained pocket watch.)

KAOMI

I respectfully request that you avoid fretting, my king. You've still some time left to appear on that harbor, do you not?

KAUIKEAOULI

The Queen Regent shall have me appear on the luakini for this!

KAPILI

Worry not, Your Majesty! I shall offer myself up as a sacrifice in your stead!

KAOMI

I humbly urge you to cease your teasing! Your Majesty is quite privy to the degree of offense Kuhina Nui Kaʻahumanu would take to such glib expressions, particularly those associating her with traditions considered by many to be barbaric.

KAUIKEAOULI

Fear not, Kaomi. The wildfire of our Lord's Word spreads far and wide, and soon ash is all that shall remain of our sinful roots.

KAOMI

The noble man is dignified, not proud to speak the Lord's name with such sardonic vigor.

KAUIKEAOULI

Ah, suddenly I am man again. Whatever could have re-mortalized me, I wonder? Doth the throne no longer put between us an excess of latitude?

KAOMI

Royal status is far from the sole barrier between our fingertips, a fact of which you must already be painfully aware.

KAUIKEAOULI

Then for now I bid you adieu, Reverend Kaomi, to avoid adding tardiness to my scripture of transgressions.

(KAUIKEAOULI runs offstage. He runs back quickly to embrace KAOMI and give him a honi ihu. KAPILI chases after him.)

SCENE 2

A large crowd gathers around the Keawaiki Brick Palace grounds. KA'AHUMANU stands behind the front palace doors, looking through the windows anxiously, surrounded by KĪNA'U, a couple of other Ali'i, and the royal guard.

KA'AHUMANU

Why oh why do my children stir my stomach so? This na'au has grown evermore nauseous with every churning.

KĪNA'U

Perhaps some grace could be granted for the king who was dropped from cradle to throne with little cushion.

KA'AHUMANU

Oh Kīna'u . . . the compulsory shield with which you shade your brother will shroud him only in darkness.

KĪNA'U

You must then pardon my desire to protect some modicum of his innocence.

KAʻAHUMANU

I regret to inform you that as Queen Regent, I am under no obligation to pardon any desires. Especially his desire to force this kingdom to wait on him hand and foot.

KĪNAʻU

Then perhaps you shan't lodge complaints concerning the adolescence of his reign.

KAʻAHUMANU

I am his mother. Were I to cease lodging complaints, many would wonder if any love for him I truly have after all.

(KAʻAHUMANU glares at KĪNAʻU. KAUIKEAOULI bursts in from the back of the palace. The royal guard gapes at him, confused and stressed, some of them putting their faces in their palms.)

KAUIKEAOULI

My deepest and most heartfelt apologies.

KAʻAHUMANU

'Tis not I you should direct those apologies toward, but to God, and our people.

KAUIKEAOULI

That could prove cumbersome, as I seldom limit my communications to a singular God.

KAPILI

Queen Regent Kaʻahumanu, I beg of you not to hold any ill will against King Kauikeaouli! His lateness was due to my failure to remind him of the address! Any punishment I will happily endure, especially involving excruciating pain or death!

(KAʻAHUMANU does not acknowledge KAPILI and instead glares at KAUIKEAOULI and walks away.)

KAUIKEAOULI

How mighty sensitive the Queen Regent has grown through this conversion.

KĪNAʻU

Ah yes, a bolt from the great beyond the sensitivity of our mother is.

KAUIKEAOULI

’Tis less shock that I am shaking with, rather than pangs of aggravation.

KĪNAʻU

She is of the belief that I exhibit insufficient strictness in regards to your should-be-expected misdeeds.

KAUIKEAOULI

She may be right. A sister is much preferable to an eternal cavalry.

KĪNAʻU

Yet unaware I am of any mutual exclusivity between those two things. But if my protection aggravates you so. . . .

KAUIKEAOULI

Greatly would I prefer words not to be placed in my mouth.

KĪNAʻU

Then this is perchance not the most ideal of occupations for my volatile little brother to continue pursuit of.

KAUIKEAOULI

Would that someone informed me of that prior to my birth into this royal ʻohana.

KĪNAʻU

My apologies. ’Tis not as if what little choice you’ve had in the matter escapes my memories.

KAUIKEAOULI

Ah, "little" carries the implication of *any* choice prior to my entrance to the throne room.

(KAUIKEAOULI walks down the palace steps.)

KAUIKEAOULI

Welina mai, my beloved people. Within an extraordinary age do we reside, in which our islands and our world undergo endless transformations, as did the islands from whence they were molded by Papahanaumoku and pulled out of the ocean by Maui. As we welcome in the days of new with arms open wide, within that embrace we should keep our ancestors as well. Unable we are to move forward without reflecting behind us. Unable we are to outrun our ever-growing crowd of exalted loved ones watching over us. Unable we are to truly forget the roots beneath our feet, singed and slashed though they may be. Unable the great nation of Hawaii is to lose its core.

SCENE 3

Music, laughter, shouting (friendly and unfriendly alike), the sound of smacking skin, and other noises fill the air, reverberating off the walls of KAUIKEAOULI's house. KAUIKEAOULI meanders excitedly through a sea of mingling people, predominantly kanaka. LILIHA enters the party holding a wooden plate of kulolo and wearing a smug grin.

LILIHA

Ah, a great hero's welcome to His Highness, the Royal Rascal.

KAUIKEAOULI

My naʻau overflows with its usual appreciation for your mockery.

LILIHA

My apologies, sir ali'i nui. 'Tis just, with such a voluminous shadow, there is no wonder none can refrain from stepping on it.

KAUIKEAOULI

Perhaps the great O'ahu Governor Kuini Liliha is more suited for comedy than politics.

BOKI

A trait yourself and my wife appear to share. . . .

KAUIKEAOULI

Perhaps you belong not to your post either, Governor Boki, considering your inability to be impartial.

LILIHA

Ah, the tragedy of the boy king.

BOKI

Please, I've not been governor for years; 'tis my wife who solely holds that title today.

KAUIKEAOULI

Within my na'au, you shall both forever govern this island. I also believe my empty palm's in need of an 'awa cup to wrap around.

(KAOMI arrives with a large keg of rum, catching KAUIKEAOULI's eye instantly.)

KAUIKEAOULI

Or perhaps I need . . . something of superior strength.

(KAUIKEAOULI walks up to KAOMI flirtatiously, grabbing a cup and starting to fill it.)

KAOMI

Aloha mai, my king.

KAUIKEAOULI

No more impeccable could your timing be, Kaomi.

KAOMI

E kalamai, but I must respectfully ask if it is advisable to imbibe so blithely in a sea of mixed company?

KAUIKEAOULI

At first sight the Queen Regent is nowhere to be found, and so goes the clearing of the coast.

KAOMI

Stifle your tongue; her servants may very well be within earshot.

KAUIKEAOULI

I grow ever so doubtful that they shall retain many memories upon tasting this beverage.

LILIHA

Ah, Kaomi, my priest and savior.

(LILIHA starts to fill a cup with rum.)

KAOMI

Kuini Liliha, how do you do as of late?

(She takes a huge swig.)

LILIHA

Much better, presently.

BOKI

All right, Liliha, you have more than showcased your liquor-grasping skills.

LILIHA

'Tis an attempt to savor every drop before Kaʻahumanu the Great ventures to tear the bottle from my fingertips.

BOKI

Come now, my love. Private quarters free of prying ears are much preferable venues for such bitterness.

KAUIKEAOULI

Fret not; we shall hold Kaomi's liquor responsible for any babblings.

KAOMI

E Kala mai?! I beg with great deference for you to pardon my ears that are yet unpleased at the sound of this plan.

(Screams can suddenly be heard by several people in the crowd. KAPILI has fainted. KAOMI rushes to his side immediately, while everyone else gathers in concern. KAOMI puts his hand on KAPILI's forehead and his other hand on his chest. His hand then moves down to KAPILI's abdomen.)

KAOMI

It appears his liver may be poisoned. He could very well pass if not treated imminently.

(KAOMI whispers prayers while holding KAPILI's stomach. A few moments pass and KAPILI jolts awake suddenly.)

BOKI

The student has become the healer! My haumana fills me with pride.

KAOMI

Quite blessed am I with guidance from great minds, e Kumu Boki.

LILIHA

We are all blessed, but most of us carry within our palms none of Akua's light.

KAOMI

You are exceedingly kind, Kuini Liliha, but merely a vessel am I.

KAPILI

Reverend Kaomi . . . while much content I was with shuffling off this mortal coil to be taken to the realm of Milu, words are surely insufficient to express my gratefulness. Perhaps flogging myself with kapa would be more—

KAOMI

Your overwhelming praise is quite much more than enough, Kapili! I graciously beg that you attempt not the showing of any further appreciation.

*(*KEKŪANAŌ'A *claps sardonically.)*

KEKŪANAŌ'A

How blessed we are that a life was saved with the archaic arts, for otherwise, simply brandishing your feathers you would have been.

KAOMI

With much due regard, Kekūanaō'a, much confusion I feel at your words. No feathers am I attempting to brandish; I simply wished to help a man in need.

KEKŪANAŌ'A

You have given yourself to the Christian God, and thus the old ways of healing should be put behind you.

KAOMI

My allowance of this man's death, I do not believe, was The Lord's wish.

KAUIKEAOULI

Kekūanaō'a, do not assume your closeness with my late and great father grants you rights to terrorize a man of God who happens to be my dear friend.

KEKŪANAŌ'A

Your Majesty.

*(*KEKŪANAŌʻA *storms out in a way he thinks to be majestic as* LILIHA *and* BOKI *laugh and start refilling their cups.* KAUIKEAOULI *stands there, staring in awe at* KAOMI*. Catching his eye,* KAOMI *smiles shyly back.)*

KAOMI
I humbly ask why the chiefly stare may be directed my way, my king.

KAUIKEAOULI
You are a true wonder, Kaomi.

KAOMI
Your Majesty.

SCENE 4

KAOMI *comes out of* KAUIKEAOULI*'s house in the morning and is surprised to see* HIRAM *walking by.*

HIRAM
Greetings, Reverend Kaomi.

KAOMI
Royal Advisor Bingham, sir.

HIRAM
Now, now, my blessed exemplar should feel free to forgo such formalities in my presence.

KAOMI
Much am I overwhelmed by the honor bestowed by you, sir. Solely with your grace and guidance have I advanced thus far.

HIRAM
I think it best you become accustomed to being overwhelmed then, as within your palm you hold the soul of every man, woman, and child in

these blessed Sandwich Isles. Sooner than you could think, honor will envelop your being.

KAOMI

My greatest efforts shall I set forth so that each and every ounce of aforementioned honor I may earn, Royal Advisor Bingham.

HIRAM

I find myself particularly relieved to see the great young king opening his ears so widely to your preachings. Some have worried he may stray a tad far from the path to heaven at times. I do much appreciate you putting those worries to eternal rest.

KAOMI

Respectfully and with reverence, it is no belief of mine that a disproportionate amount of steps have been veered from the path our Lord has carved for his majesty. I am certain it is not my place to say, but with the illuminating glow of youth, much motion is brought, and thus a stumble here, a stumble there exists not beyond expectation.

HIRAM

I deeply admire your admiration for the young Kamehameha, as well as your need to speak of your true feelings, misguided as they may be.

KAOMI

My deepest apologies, for why my awareness of the out-of-turn manner in which I was speaking instilled within me no restraint is utterly confounding.

HIRAM

Nonsense. Were Christ himself not to test the waters, however would he have known he could walk on them?

KAOMI

To the prodigal son I am worthy of no comparison. Moreover, the great Royal Advisor from whom I have been imparted endless knowledge of literature and scripture alike should be subject to no tests from myself. For your forgiveness I humbly beg.

(BOKI walks up from behind KAOMI.)

BOKI

But it is not he alone from whom you've gained *all* knowledge now, is it?

(KAOMI jumps, surprised, then smiles when he turns around and sees BOKI behind him.)

KAOMI

My apologies for my reaction, Kumu Boki. I was nearly provided a fainting spell due to your sudden appearance.

HIRAM

Don't you think it unbecoming for a preacher of God's word to be so easily frightened?

BOKI

Must you scold him so absurdly, Hiram?

HIRAM

Former Governor Boki, it appears you've suffered a lapse in memory in regards to where your respect should be paid.

BOKI

I merely suggest you ease up on Kaomi, as he's a powerful individual equally deserving of that respect.

HIRAM

Indeed. Kaomi here is now a priest at Lahaina's largest church. Whilst you and your court spew blasphemous riddles as you please, Kaomi has been granted a heavenly burden. His words carry with him the weight of God himself.

BOKI

I never tire of speaking to this man. He is so effortlessly amusing.

HIRAM

And it's thusly of great importance that his focus not stray from the light at the end of the Lord's tunnel.

BOKI

Kaomi is attached to the house of Kaʻahumanu, after all. I'd assert this man has garnered more chiefly experience than most. Certainly more than some in this room.

(KAOMI stands between them nervously.)

KAOMI

Please, you two, it is no place of mine to intervene but I must respectfully remind you both that this is no Colosseum! I've had more than my share of internal conflict without my two most influential educators holding blades to each other's necks.

HIRAM

May the Lord continue to bestow his blessings upon you. . . .

BOKI

Mahalo Nui loa Hiram.

SCENE 5

KAʻAHUMANU gives an address on the steps of Keawaʻiki Brick Palace as KAOMI dances hula flirtatiously for KAUIKEAOULI.

KAʻAHUMANU

Among the proudest traits of the Hawaiian people is our ability to adapt. While many long deeply for the days of old, much importance there is in remembering the pool of blood that need not have risen over the centuries. The days of newcomers may frighten many, but they may provide our only means to evade drowning in the rising red tide. The hands on the pocket watch we have been given doth not turn backwards.

Tragically and sorely misguided were our ancestors, wise as they may have been. Multitudes of unnecessary losses have we suffered, at the bloody hands of a barbaric kapu system. At the wrong hands which unbelievable power fell into. At the hands of chiefs who cared not of the lives of their people, so long as their reign remained the axis upon which those lives revolved. But it is my true and concrete belief that united under one God, our loved ones shall no longer be so swiftly expedited to the heavens.

Blessed we have been with the opportunity to repent for our ancestors' mistakes. We who have been spared of the many plagues, we who have crossed to the correct side of bayonets, we who have been united by my late and great husband King Kamehameha: we are the chosen, and it is our time to walk into the light ahead.

SCENE 6

KA'AHUMANU and HIRAM play chess in KA'AHUMANU's home.

HIRAM

The great ali'i, Kaikio'ewa, has voiced much distress in regards to your son's recent recklessness, and in his words, your inability to force the king into line.

KA'AHUMANU

I would be quite intrigued to witness a demonstration of fatherhood by the great Kaua'i Governor. The invitation remains wide open to try his own hand at wrangling the boy king.

HIRAM

I also advised him to keep an eye fixed on that mouth of his whilst speaking of the great Queen Regent.

KAʻAHUMANU
My apologies, Advisor Bingham. Further restraint in voicing my disdain would be advisable.

HIRAM
Your hanai son is quite fond of my student and exemplar, Reverend Kaomi, is he not?

KAʻAHUMANU
Ah yes. Kauikeaouli and Kaomi have found much kinship in each other. Why is it that you ask?

HIRAM
Oh it's but a small observation I have made. . . .

KAʻAHUMANU
'Tis no custom of mine to perceive any observation of my royal advisor's as small.

HIRAM
I merely wonder if perhaps what the young Kamehameha shows Reverend Kaomi is beyond mere fondness and kinship. . . .

(KAʻAHUMANU is quiet for a moment.)

HIRAM
Now, I'm aware that many of the Hawaiian royalty chose to engage in some archaic traditions that are not aligned with those of the Church. And that is something I have been more than willing to avoid peering too closely at. Kaomi, however, is a man of God. And furthermore, I am doubtful a man of his confounding heritage exhibiting such proximity to the king would be received well by the Hawaiian people.

(KAʻAHUMANU's silence becomes louder as HIRAM puts his rook dangerously near KAʻAHUMANU's king, threatening to put her in check. KAʻAHUMANU pulls her king out of danger at the last second.)

HIRAM

Ah, I've worried you unnecessarily; please forgive me, Queen Regent.

KA'AHUMANU

Nonsense, it's of utmost importance that you always speak truthfully with me, and greatly appreciated nonetheless.

HIRAM

But I shouldn't add rum to a fire already burning in your mind. What with the stress you undergo in the aftermath of the king's gathering—

KA'AHUMANU

What gathering?

HIRAM

Oh, my apologies once more, I should've presumed the king would prevent any messengers from reaching you.

KA'AHUMANU

And why might he do such a thing?

(HIRAM finally succeeds in putting KA'AHUMANU in check.)

HIRAM

Nay, it's unbecoming for a man in my position to engage in such idle gossip. Especially tall tales of the overconsumption of distilled liquor provided by Reverend Kaomi. It is best we deafen our ears to such delusional whispers.

(KA'AHUMANU drops her king before she is able to move him out of check.)

KA'AHUMANU

Advisor Bingham, if you will please excuse me. . . .

HIRAM

Your Highness.

SCENE 7

KAʻAHUMANU storms into KĪNAʻU's chambers.

KĪNAʻU

Whatever has worked my mother into such a gust?

KAʻAHUMANU

A plethora of ʻaikāne to choose from, and that brother of yours has to play with the lord's guiding flame.

KĪNAʻU

I beg that you pardon my lack of immediate understanding.

KAʻAHUMANU

Hiram Bingham seems to have grown suspicious in regards to Kauikeaouli's devotion to the church, and one of its leaders in particular.

KĪNAʻU

Kaomi? 'Tis quite unlike you to jest so heavily, mother.

KAʻAHUMANU

Does he truly think this conversion has been but a serene breeze?! Does he think lightly of the doing of what I need to ensure the protection of our people?!

KĪNAʻU

This is in earnest?? Is Kaomi not Bingham's student? And let us not evade the minor detail that he is a Protestant minister... that he would show such infidelity to his Lord appears greatly doubtful.

KAʻAHUMANU

What a wonder it is that you may gain such amusement from the summoning of the Rapture.

KĪNAʻU

Ah yes, the Four Horsemen shall each be stationed at the furthermost corners of this island.

KAʻAHUMANU

I am not speaking of a sequel to the Book of Revelation! I am speaking of the rapture the missionaries would create were a man of their word to take up with the king himself!

KĪNAʻU

Quite aware I am of the bayonets at our throats. Ah yes, I have an idea. Allow your children to complete puberty before thrusting them into the spotlit puppeteer's chair.

KAʻAHUMANU

I've grown deeply exhausted by your lack of deference, as well as your eternal stream of excuses for him! None of us were permitted to be children before receiving the reins. Your beloved brother, whom you keep shaded beneath your wing, should be no exception. And if you are indeed so aware of this nation's stakes, then why do you seem yet unconcerned?

KĪNAʻU

I've as of yet seen nothing sufficiently concrete to stoke my flames of fear.

KAʻAHUMANU

"The king twirls bedsheets betwixt political ideologies with a half-caste priest!" they will whisper across crowds.

(KĪNAʻU looks concerned.)

KĪNAʻU

Quite difficult I find it to justify adherence to the mere potential of whispers.

KAʻAHUMANU

Forget not Manono and Kuamoʻo. Do you wish the same bloodbath upon your brother? Upon Kaomi? Upon this nation?

SCENE 8

KAUIKEAOULI dances hula by himself in his large room, which KAʻAHUMANU somewhat hesitantly walks into.

KAʻAHUMANU

Some stories have been tickling my ear as of late.

KAUIKEAOULI

Regarding which topics, I wonder. . . .

KAʻAHUMANU

Included subjects featured some interesting theories in regards to your relationship with Kaomi. I've known you two to be close, but I suppose the extent of said closeness still exceeds my knowledge.

KAUIKEAOULI

It seems unlike you to believe whispers carried across the hau vine, Mother.

KAʻAHUMANU

'Twas not from the hau vine, but from my Royal Advisor himself.

KAUIKEAOULI

Ah, yes, 'tis a world-famous fact that haole missionaries are the utmost trustworthy of individuals.

KAʻAHUMANU

It would be my great preference for you to avoid feigning ignorance, Kauikeaouli. Gaggles of kāne crowd the palace steps, awaiting your gaze, yet the man in the pulpit is whom you elect to lock eyes with.

KAUIKEAOULI

May I please be permitted to foster friendships, O Queen Mother Regent?

KAʻAHUMANU

’Tis clear as unclouded moonlight that you and Reverend Kaomi are more than kindred spirits.

KAUIKEAOULI

I shan’t pretend to believe this is truly about my “sinful pleasures.”

KAʻAHUMANU

I spoke nothing of sin. You are aware of the multitudes of women who’ve shared my bed. Yet I at least have the good taste not to bed the clergy.

KAUIKEAOULI

I believe your true concern lies in my allergy to servitude being contagious.

(KAʻAHUMANU looks forward, not at KAUIKEAOULI, coldly and firmly.)

KAʻAHUMANU

My true concern lies in watching a child under my care hurl himself into a den of lions in such a cavalier manner! It is a strong wish of mine that many years you are to outlive me.

KAUIKEAOULI

Well it is a strong wish of mine that the culture of our people long outlive the both of us!

KAʻAHUMANU

The American Board of Commissioners for Foreign Missions will already be angry with Kaomi’s companionship to any man other than God. But furthermore, he has begun to exhibit unsavory attitudes towards Advisor Bingham, as well as others in the Church.

KAUIKEAOULI

Aww, my naʻau has never been filled with such ha’aheo. Pride bursts from my veins.

KAʻAHUMANU

Well it should be filled with hilahila! Your casual subversion of recently instilled liquor laws and Christian ideals is enough of an endangerment to the house of cards we've painstakingly built. But moreover, Kaomi is a good boy, and it is imperative to our kingdom that he remain that way!

KAUIKEAOULI

So I gather that the trade was worth it, then? Abolishing the kapu system for a new set of chains?

KAʻAHUMANU

The Church's infrastructure does at the very least allow you to rebel in such ways without being put to death.

KAUIKEAOULI

The way you speak suggests otherwise.

KAʻAHUMANU

Think of Kaomi. Think of how such a scandal could cause his church to crumble, crushing him before he can reach the inward-opening doors. Think of how a relationship with the king could shine an excess of sunlight onto his complexion! Or have you forgotten the way in which half-castes in this kingdom are looked upon?

KAUIKEAOULI

Do not refer to him that way! Were our ancestors so afraid of the mixing of blood, our existence would be void! If their power you wish to abolish, that is a wish I have no desire to assist in fulfilling.

KAʻAHUMANU

How dare you! 'Tis that power that I am trying to fulfill in order to save our people!

KAUIKEAOULI

And what utterly superb progress you have made. Our people are simply thriving!

(KA'AHUMANU suddenly grabs her stomach, in extreme pain.)

KAUIKEAOULI
Queen Regent?!

(KA'AHUMANU falls to the floor and KAUIKEAOULI runs to her side, helping to hold her up.)

KAUIKEAOULI
Mama! Please, what is ailing you so?!

(KA'AHUMANU screams out. KAUIKEAOULI storms off toward the palace gates.)

SCENE 9

KAUIKEAOULI paces back and forth through the hallway outside KA'AHUMANU's room, where KAOMI and BOKI are attending to her. KAOMI touches KA'AHUMANU's forehead and looks concerned. At his touch she smiles and sits up. KAOMI exits the room.

KAUIKEAOULI
Kaomi, I beg of you to tell me your diagnosis differs from the fearmongering of these haole doctors.

KAOMI
I am afraid the sole distinction is how far worse her intestinal illness has progressed.

(KAOMI puts his hand on KAUIKEAOULI's shoulder.)

KAUIKEAOULI
This cannot be... she was just berating me mere moments ago....

(BOKI also comes out of the room.)

KAUIKEAOULI

Please, Boki. Kaomi. You are both masters in the arts of healing. This illness is highly reversible, is it not?

(BOKI looks down.)

KAUIKEAOULI

Whatever is the matter with the two of you? Are you both possessed at the hands of ʻuhane who are content with giving up?!

BOKI

Do you think for even a moment that it pains neither of us to shatter this news?

(KAUIKEAOULI storms over to KAʻAHUMANU's bed. KAPILI tries to stop him.)

KAPILI

Please, sir, I beg of you not to disturb the Queen Regent. She has requested that you specifically avoid her bedside for fear of annoyance. My apologies, instructed to repeat that I was not.

KAUIKEAOULI

Kapili, if you do not clear the way, I shall have you put to death.

KAPILI

Yes, Your Majesty. Or if it would be your prerogative I could put myself to death so as not to tire your already worn hands.

KAUIKEAOULI

I . . . I must apologize. I would not truly put you to death. I know not of why I stated that. I am merely in a foul mood.

KAPILI

No, no, Your Majesty, no apologies are necessary! The offer to complete the deed myself remains open! I live and potentially die but to serve.

KAUIKEAOULI

You are a blessing on this great kingdom, Kapili.

(KAUIKEAOULI continues walking over to KAʻAHUMANU's side.)

KAʻAHUMANU

This is highly unbecoming behavior of a young king, and more pertinently, it brings me great annoyance. I demand that you leave my side at once.

KAUIKEAOULI

All the power of the nation at my fingertips must amount to the mana that would be taken to save you.

KAʻAHUMANU

I trust that in capable hands I am leaving this kingdom.

KAUIKEAOULI

The impression I was given from our previous conversation differed much from that notion!

KAʻAHUMANU

I am aware that you are quite adept at listening to your naʻau, but you must also listen to your poʻo. A king must be as level-headed as he is passionate. He must place the needs of his people, of his nation, above his own desires. Sway not the boat too heavily or we shall all soon be capsized. Much bloodshed and anguish we have faced because of those before you who believed that within their own hands they could take this nation, with little forethought of other hands shaping it and those being shapen. It is you who must bring us into the future, or at the very least, you must ensure that a future to look forward to exists within our grasp. And to do so, you must cease this cycle, and become the history that repeats not. At times that means moving with the flow, even from whence the stream is diverted by manmade structures.

(KAUIKEAOULI runs out of the room, crying.)

SCENE 10

KAUIKEAOULI sits on the beach near where Aloha Tower is now, staring out into the ocean. KAOMI walks up behind him.

KAUIKEAOULI

I wish to be left alone at the moment, Reverend Kaomi.

KAOMI

It is my wish for my king to care for himself.

KAUIKEAOULI

I would be delighted if you stopped referring to me thusly. As you view me not as a mere friend, I do view you not as a mere subject.

KAOMI

If I may show such boldness, much kanalua do I feel within you. 'Tis imperative that you stop blaming yourself for the illness of Kuhina Nui Ka'ahumanu.

KAUIKEAOULI

Whilst much do I admire the power of your bodily perception and healing ability, I would ask that you refrain from delving deeper into my na'au.

(KAUIKEAOULI is silent.)

KAOMI

In that regard, the only skills I possess have been passed down to me from Kumu Boki, and even those are incapable of reversing illness.

(KAOMI starts to cry.)

KAOMI

None but a useless half-caste from Lahaina I am. I've no business preaching the word of God, nor do I have any business engaging so deeply with royalty.

(KAOMI stands up to leave.)

KAOMI

One wish that I'm capable of fulfilling I shall grant and thus I shall leave you be. E kala mai.

(KAOMI starts to walk away. KAUIKEAOULI reaches out to him longingly before he can leave.)

KAUIKEAOULI

Kaomi! Please . . . do not leave my side. My deepest apologies for brushing you away like old kukui leaves . . . I mustn't mourn in such a way that wounds you whilst you attempt to lift my heavy spirits.

KAOMI

'Tis no matter anyhow. I feel as though I am unfit to preach the word of God when I carry less belief in his words advancing forth from my mouth with each passing day. Would a minister of higher purity deliver those words, perhaps the ears they fall upon would not be deafened. It sometimes feels as though my ancestors, split by oceans, are not in agreement with the scripture I must uphold.

KAUIKEAOULI

Would it interest you to learn an unsavory secret of mine?

(KAUIKEAOULI grasps KAOMI's hand firmly.)

KAUIKEAOULI

I live in perpetual terror.

KAOMI

Your Maje—

KAUIKEAOULI

Every moment seated in that unfooted chair they call a throne, waves of icy fear are sent through each fiber of my being. I know not what can be done to serve the people. I know not how I may please my family. I know not how to carry this kingdom on my still-growing shoulders. I grow especially wary of the near-vertical cliff I must climb whilst keeping the nation firmly hoisted upon my back. I fear my next stumble shall bring it all crashing down.

(Beat.)

KAUIKEAOULI

But I also fear what shall happen were I to fall in line. I fear the missionaries shall tie their strings tightly to each of my limbs and hula shall not be the dance I am pulled to perform. I fear becoming a king-shaped pawn, who has advanced too far what may soon be relics of our culture. I fear that our mana shall not survive this.

(Beat.)

KAUIKEAOULI

I fear that we shall lose everything. I fear that I shall lose you.

(KAUIKEAOULI grabs onto KAOMI, holding him tightly, to KAOMI's flustered surprise.)

KAOMI

Perhaps I am already lost. I am but a worthless vessel within whom the Lord has misplaced much great trust.

KAUIKEAOULI

No, you are the greatest gift he has sent us.

(KAOMI looks KAUIKEAOULI in the eye, close up.)

KAUIKEAOULI

A gift I am especially grateful for.

(KAUIKEAOULI kisses KAOMI, whose eyes remain open in shock for a few moments before he starts to kiss KAUIKEAOULI back deeply. When the kiss is over, KAUIKEAOULI walks away, leaving KAOMI in a flurry of swirling emotions.)

SCENE 11

KAOMI sits in the front pew of his church, his hands clasped in prayer.

KAOMI

E nā 'Akua. 'Tis your wisdom and forgiveness alike which I humbly seek.

I know it is no sin to love our king. He is majestic and beautiful, and it's the people's duty to love him. Frightened, however, I have become, that the love I have for him stretches beyond reverence. Afraid I am that the love growing in my na'au like a hau bush is not simply the love a commoner has for his ruler, but a greater love. A love that springs with butterflies and tidal waves rises forth. A love which seems to be accompanied by . . . something that feels much like lust.

I know that slap my wrist you all would not, for long has this been our way. Forgiveness I hope greatly that you may impart upon me for the doubt I place in you, and for my commitment to another god who wishes not to share me. I have prayed to you less and less, for fear that I shall be reprimanded for betrayal of the church roof that has given me much shelter. I wonder much as of late who is god and who is devil.

The missionaries tell me that my love for Kauikeaouli is one of many plagues decimating our people. But then I do not understand. 'Tis doubtful I am the first man the king has looked upon in this manner. Were this a plague, for many centuries have our kings and queens along with the multitudes been infected. Were this a plague, the gods I pray to, you all, are the original carriers. And that may be the singular belief I find difficult to grasp. For the arrows of the Almighty are within me, The poison whereof my spirit drinketh up: The terrors of God do set themselves in array against me.

Or perhaps, this is neither devil nor plague. Perhaps this is no curse, but the latest of your blessings. In which case, someone should surely inform your followers.

SCENE 12

KAUIKEAOULI walks into KAʻAHUMANU's Mānoa home. She lies in her bed, sickly.

KAUIKEAOULI

Aloha mai, mother. How are you feeling?

KAʻAHUMANU

Closer and closer to the light I advance forth with each passing day.

KAUIKEAOULI

It is my great wish that the power to hold you from that light were within my grasp.

KAʻAHUMANU

Perhaps this country you also wish to hold back from the light of Christ. But it shall shine regardless.

KAUIKEAOULI

I had not realized that it was Christ's light we were speaking of.

KAʻAHUMANU

It has become clear that you are unable to tend to this nation with none at your side.

KAUIKEAOULI

I am in fierce agreement with that notion. For which reason I have decided to bring Kaomi on as my mōʻī-kuʻi.

KAʻAHUMANU

Nonsense! Kaomi may not serve as your engrafted king! Is this how strongly you desire to paint the palace walls in blood?

KAUIKEAOULI

My desire lies in the great nation of Hawaii having its innards not forcibly removed.

KAʻAHUMANU

There are inevitabilities you must accept. Such as the inevitable need for the king to have a Hawaiian woman by his side.

KAUIKEAOULI

There are many dying wishes I may be willing to grant, but donning a decorative bride is far beyond the confines of that list.

KAʻAHUMANU

You carry my late husband's name, and with it his legacy. If he'd had no pure queen at his side, he'd furthermore have had no guns, no army, and no palace to keep them in. Thus you shall meet with this young chiefess and take her on as your wife.

KAUIKEAOULI

And what might this lovely young woman's feelings be regarding her existence as a political pawn?

KAʻAHUMANU

It seems you lack understanding of the game of chess, as much difference in power exists between pawns and queens.

KAUIKEAOULI

And what of Kaomi? Shall I discard him like rotten kalo?

KAʻAHUMANU

It is not I who has deemed Kaomi a half-caste! The minds of those who hold purity in the highest regard I cannot change! Furthermore, I worry that Kaomi may find difficulty in balancing his dedication to God's work with his dedication towards you and your plan to topple this nation. Even were you to simply take him on as a lover, were you to refrain shouting it from each mountain top, it could be of slightly lesser calamity.

KAUIKEAOULI

I am the king. If my choice in ʻaikāne partners conflict with the emotions of certain clergy members, they must search deeply within their pure hearts for a proper method of endurance. Requested power this was not. Thirst for the throne I did not. Yet I was placed in it anyhow, and so, anyone with whom I elect to share it shall be welcomed.

(KAʻAHUMANU starts coughing heavily.)

KAʻAHUMANU

Look upon me, Kauikeaouli. Soon I shall no longer be able to lead this kingdom. Soon I, like many of our people, shall become a part of the ʻāina, and I must know that the hands I am leaving this kingdom in will hold it firmly!

KAUIKEAOULI

I fail to see why those hands can hold the kingdom but not the man I love the most.

KAʻAHUMANU

Was it not you who put forth the law that any commoner who has committed sexual misconduct must be punished by hard labor?

KAUIKEAOULI

Not included in that decree were our traditional forms of love. Traditions I shall remind you that you once practiced.

KAʻAHUMANU

I declined to practice them in such a frivolous manner! None of the wahine with whom I was intimate were spoken for by God. None of the women I invited into my bed shared my command. None of my women stood upon a fissure in the foundation of this country!

KAUIKEAOULI

Then it is decided. I shall put myself to hard labor in accordance with the letter of my own law, if that is what you so desire.

KAʻAHUMANU

What I desire is for you to treat both the throne and the life you've been given with proper respect, not to behave like a commoner to belabor the point.

KAUIKEAOULI

Much would I prefer my body to never feel a moment's rest than to marry a woman I know not. I should much rather work without pause, until my hands fall to pieces like old, eroded rocks on the side of Kapaʻa.

KAʻAHUMANU

If you fail to be careful, the haole will cut those hands off and take the kingdom for themselves! Many including yourself believe that I swore the nation to the church to indoctrinate our people into my modern beliefs. But I did it to save us. And that I shall continue until my dying breath.

KAUIKEAOULI

As will I, mother.

(KAUIKEAOULI walks out of the room angrily.)

SCENE 13

KAUIKEAOULI hammers away at a fence he is building alongside KAPILI for HIRAM as the sun quickly moves from east to west, sets and rises, repeatedly. KAUIKEAOULI keeps working nonstop through light and dark. HIRAM walks by and exchanges stares with KAUIKEAOULI, who continues to labor away.

SCENE 14

KAOMI, whose eyes are nervously closed, is led down a mysterious hallway by KAUIKEAOULI.

KAOMI
I respectfully hope this surprise lives up to the anxiety it's stirred within me.

KAUIKEAOULI
Fear not, e ku'u ipo 'tis a surprise worth dying for.

KAOMI
If you continue referring to me affectionately, that death may be ensured.

KAUIKEAOULI
There is no need for dramatics.

KAOMI
Spoke the man leading me blindly.

(They arrive at a wooden door, which KAUIKEAOULI opens and leads KAOMI through.)

KAUIKEAOULI
You may feel at leisure to open your eyes, Kaomi.

(KAOMI opens his eyes nervously and is immediately confused and looks around a large room.)

KAOMI
With all due respect, Your Majesty, I have not the clarity as to what your great surprise is.

KAUIKEAOULI
The working space of the hulumanu.

KAUIKEAOULI

Like the elepaio, and many other of our birds, the Hawaiian culture and people are facing extinction. And between the ABCFM and the great royal ʻohana from which I hail, that extinction is being expedited tremendously.

KAOMI

You must forgive my lack of certainty as to where I fit into this equation.

KAUIKEAOULI

Alongside your love and compassion, you have inspired me to move against the whitened grain. The true meaning of pono has become lost amongst our people, redefined by haole missionaries to fit what God in their Bible deem as righteous. However, much like the ʻālaeʻula, a spark you have lit within me within me. That spark has grown into a raging fire within my naʻau, which I strive to use to warm this nation up once again, and rekindle its life.

KAOMI

Many emotions fill me to the brim, including honor and dread alike. I must respectfully ask, do you forget that I myself am a man of the Christian God? I preach the word that fire in you is urged to burn.

KAUIKEAOULI

That is even more reason, my Kaomi. Each of your feet step forward on the paths to both spiritual worlds. You are living proof that our ancestors may coexist with his angels yet.

KAOMI

I shall only be living proof for so long if not careful.

KAUIKEAOULI

Feathers may be light but this decision is not, and it is yours to make once you're ready. We shall seldom be written of in history books, as those quills reside between poised white fingers . . . nonetheless, history is what we shall make.

KAUIKEAOULI

So, Kaomi . . . .

(KAUIKEAOULI reaches his hand out to KAOMI.)

KAUIKEAOULI

Would you like to join me in reviving this great nation?

SCENE 15

Another party is happening at KAUIKEAOULI's house, this time more raucous and joyful. Many are dancing hula, others play Makahiki games. LILIHA sits with KAUIKEAOULI, both of them drinking.

LILIHA

The Queen Regent attempted to offer you a bride?? Is there a seafloor to the depths of her Protestant delusions?

KAUIKEAOULI

The ocean is endless.

LILIHA

I've much respect for Kuhina Nui Ka'ahumanu, conflicted and kanalua as my feelings are. This, however, leaves me utterly appalled.

KAUIKEAOULI

If my hanai mother wishes to force my hand in marriage, she must hold a leiomano to my throat.

LILIHA

I feel doubtful that she would utilize weapons not ordained by the Church.

KAUIKEAOULI

Then no wonder it is that she seems to have no qualms with utilizing mine own guilt to the content of her na'au.

(LILIHA gets up and walks outside. She sees KAOMI sitting on the mansion steps.)

LILIHA

For what reason have I found you out here, e Kaomi? Whatever became of basking in your king's glorious affection?

KAOMI

Forgive me, Kuini Liliha, but as of this moment, I am content with basking in the moonlight.

LILIHA

A commendable choice indeed, but I still wonder what has you so sullen?

KAOMI

No intention of mine is to threaten the great king's reign, or worse, his life.

LILIHA

Well, fortunately that burden falls upon the shoulders of Queen Regent Kaʻahumanu.

KAOMI

I with great humility disagree, Kuini Liliha. It is I who is the burden. And quite a weighted burden I am.

LILIHA

'Tis my deep belief that even you are aware of how untrue those words are.

(LILIHA sits down next to KAOMI.)

LILIHA

Kaʻahumanu, with all of her beauty, grace, and strength, has been deeply afflicted by illness.

KAOMI

Sorrow has filled each fiber of my being at the rapidly declining health of our great Kuhina Nui.

LILIHA

I speak not only of her physical ailments. I speak of the illness of her na'au, which, despite the belief of many in the royal court, has led her, and subsequently our nation, astray. While kapu have always been a part of our traditions, so has noa. Our freedom is part of the balance that has for centuries kept our people alive. Her system of " 'ainoa" may have freed us of some restrictions, at the cost of many other freedoms. The restrictions she has placed upon our traditions, such as hula, such as the building of 'ahu, such as the games of Makahiki, are hewa. Bounds from ka po'e haole, tightening ever-so-gradually, until our bones break and our breath is naught. No longer am I even allowed to practice Catholicism, for prayer to even one God shall only be given through specific vessels deemed properly righteous.

(Beat.)

LILIHA

Much more than a vessel you are, Kaomi. Infinitely more love does Kauikeaouli possess for you than respect for the haole restrictions forced upon our people, and he shall never stop fighting for that love. He even refused a bride to whom Ka'ahumanu attempted to promise him.

KAOMI

Whilst it is no place of mine to judge the choices of my king, that one does not appear the most strategic. A life of happiness he much deserves, not a life bound by this sinful half-caste who cannot choose between mine own heart and the light shining into it.

LILIHA

To my current knowledge, no life free of sin exists in this plane, especially for those of royalty.

(LILIHA hugs KAOMI from the side. KAOMI leans into the warm embrace.)

LILIHA

Now, it is imperative that I stretch my pained legs. Leave not your king for too long.

KAOMI

May I?

(He lays his hands on her legs. After a few moments, LILIHA smiles, rejuvenated and healed by his touch.)

LILIHA

Mahalo nui loa Boki, truly my savior you are.

BOKI

Much commendations for your strong spine standing up to the Kuhina Nui. 'Tis no simple feat.

KAUIKEAOULI

I fear sufficiently proper respect I failed to show her. I am perhaps an even more worthless son than king.

BOKI

Not long before, one could be put to death for speaking of the king in such a way. Whilst that is a tradition I am content with leaving behind us, I believe the disdain you hold for yourself should be forgotten as well. More than sufficient has been the punishment through which you have subjected yourself. No more would I like to watch you suffer at your own hand.

KAUIKEAOULI

The kingdom, the people, and Kaomi suffer greatly at my hand. Much understanding I lack for why I alone should be spared.

BOKI

If I may be so bold, I've worried much about Kaomi for a long while. While my teachings in the arts of healing have their flaws, I have instructed him to my best ability. But I've worried about the pale hands that have had their turn of molding his mana'o. I've worried much of his straying from his path to a path lit in white light.... A path that leaves him drowning in hatred of his own na'au. So it fills me with pride and delight to see him find love with someone who provides him the same healing he provides those around him.

KAUIKEAOULI

I am without words, only gratitude.

KAOMI

If I may be so emboldened to ask, where might Your Majesty be gallivanting off to?

KAUIKEAOULI

'Tis a true treat to be granted mine own personal royal guard to have and to hold.

KAOMI

Respectfully, Your Majesty exhibits much more adeptness in shaking the royal guard than shaking me.

KAUIKEAOULI

Would you like to put the notion to the test?

(KAOMI blushes. KAUIKEAOULI kisses him. Suddenly, they are surrounded by KĪNA'U, KEKŪANAŌ'A and several members of the royal guard.)

KAUIKEAOULI

You must return inside and blockade each door. Instantly!

KAOMI

O-of what is it that you speak?! Your Majesty, with all due consideration, I refuse to hide indoors while you are in the midst of dange—

KAUIKEAOULI

Your king just gave you an order, Kaomi, and it would be much preferable not to repeat myself.

(KAOMI stands in shock momentarily and walks inside at once.)

KĪNAʻU

You've no awareness of how exhausting a task can become of attempting to protect you and our people simultaneously. 'Tis not your prerogative to throw yourself to the cannons when the nation you hold in your fingertips!

KAUIKEAOULI

Whatever came of "judge not lest ye be judged?"

KĪNAʻU

Is it your true belief that I live an existence free of judgement? What an absurd dream you must live in. Naturally, it becomes my responsibility to douse that ever-smirking face in frigid water.

KAUIKEAOULI

Ah yes, because you have never been provided the touch of a woman yourself. And neither does the Queen Regent. No hereditary trait this is.

KĪNAʻU

I also wish your martyrdom would cease! You must stop painting us with a brush that knows no color!

KEKŪANAŌʻA

My wife, Kuini Kīnaʻu, shall be appointed by Kaʻahumanu as successor Kuhina Nui. Additionally, there has been a change of plan regarding your delusional appointing of this half-caste as mōʻī ku'i.

KAUIKEAOULI

I am quite amused that my late and great father's primary intimate partner would fall so deeply in love with the missionaries' reign. Or perhaps it is simply disdain you have carried for me since my childhood, which still supersedes my comprehension. 'Tis not as if I stole much of father's attention.

KEKŪANAŌʻA

You've much audacity to mention the true Kamehameha's name so blithely. No comparison exists. Your father was a true king. Only with strong necessity did he antagonize our visitors.

KAUIKEAOULI

Worry not. That he required haole assistance to conquer the islands lives strong in my memory, even if he had bloodied them so. But never did he bow down to their god, who seems to have taken ownership of others in present company.

KEKŪANAŌʻA

You know nothing of what you speak, Kauikeaouli! I urge you never again to denigrate his memory in such a way.

KAUIKEAOULI

Much curiosity I have always had, for how your presence was received by father's gun-and-Bible-toting acquaintances. Doubt somehow enters my mind that they welcomed his lover with open arms.

KEKŪANAŌʻA

I believe His Majesty's competency, strength and will more than sufficed to make up for what they may have viewed as sinful.

KAUIKEAOULI

Ah so if you hand the haoles the land grant to your soul, you may love whomever you please, is that it?

KEKŪANAŌʻA

You shouldn't dare speak this way. It may be noteworthy that I at least am a full-blooded Hawaiian, and so my place at the foot of the throne was rightfully chosen.

KAUIKEAOULI

Launch not such glib attacks upon Kaomi's ancestry. It has been no belief of mine that purity of blood a Hawaiian man makes.

KEKŪANAŌʻA

On this your opinion differs greatly from that of many of our people. That man and royalty differ greatly must also not be forgotten. And to be royal is a privilege for which purity is a prerequisite.

KĪNAʻU

We are simply asking that you demonstrate some form of discretion. And discretion includes not the blatant appointing of your ʻaikāne to a position of power. Especially from whence you've already robbed him from their church.

KEKŪANAŌʻA

On the subject of your absurd choices, upon fetching Liliha for her summons, she was found, staunchly drunken. This is whom you've chosen as a successor to Kaʻahumanu.

(Another guard walks into the house menacingly, holding LILIHA.*)*

KAUIKEAOULI

Is it your belief that treating Oahu's Royal Governor as seabourne prisoner will persuade me to accept your demands?

KĪNAʻU

It fills me with sorrow to do this, Kauikeaouli. Your safety and happiness have eternally been of utmost importance to me. But it seems both I cannot protect. Nor can I protect Kaomi along with the kingdom, unless proper deference you begin to show.

KAUIKEAOULI

I'd be quite pleased if you departed from my home at this time. I feel strangely doubtful that your presence is to the enjoyment of my house guest.

SCENE 16

KAOMI silently folds his priest hammock in the back of the church. HIRAM enters behind him.

HIRAM

And so your mind is made up in abandoning your duties to God, is it, former Reverend Kaomi?

KAOMI

Were my profuse apologies not to your satisfaction? For the knowledge you have bestowed upon me, Advisor Bingham, I shall be forever grateful. The lord is simply leading me on a path not carved out by you.

HIRAM

Don't pretend it's the lord leading you on this coarse, rocky, mountain trail you attempt to label a path. Upon the wicked he shall rain snares, fire and brimstone, and a horrible tempest, this shall be the portion of their cup.

KAOMI

Psalms 11:6, you need not test my knowledge. I have been provided a chance to attempt to save this nation, and foolish it would seem not to take it.

KĪNAʻU

Governor Liliha, to what do I owe this invasion?

LILIHA

How dare you pull this nation's rug from under it!

KĪNAʻU

My mother has entrusted that I secure that rug. Were I not to act, every fiber could catch ablaze, with missionaries and commoners stoking the flames alike.

HIRAM

You've been provided temptation, by a man wearing king's robes that do not fit no matter the tailor.

KAOMI

I have been provided with love!

HIRAM

It is I who taught you how to spell that four-letter word.

KAOMI

And to repay that debt I'll do whatever I may, but that shall never again include ignoring my naʻau.

LILIHA

While I wish not to rattle Kaʻahumanu's deathbed with these turmoils, I also approve not of your usurping of the power not held solely in your palms.

KĪNAʻU

Ah yes, the previous civil war was so serene, only further peace will come of revitalizing that bloodshed!

LILIHA

This is not Manono and Kuamoʻo! Your brother and Kaomi are staging no coup. They intend to create no upheaval!

KĪNAʻU

An innocent, heaven-made marriage between Church and monarchy, is that it? Yes I am sure the growing Calvinists will look upon their union as truly holy. No potential exists for rioting.

LILIHA

Their fate is not yours to decide!

HIRAM

Your naʻau, as you call, it is misguided! Prove yourself a doer of the word, and not merely a hearer who deludes himself.

KAOMI

James 1.22 may have been more relevant had I anything to prove.

HIRAM

Your innocence, perhaps?

KAOMI

The king's robes fit perfectly. But this priestly vestment does not. And it has begun to itch uncontrollably.

LILIHA

You may be content with your movements restricted to diagonal dashes, but I have no interest in playing by the rules of this chess game. And even if I were, it is part of my duty to protect my king from surrounding white pieces.

KĪNAʻU

That is precisely what I intend to do. Strategically we must move, for their armies are ever advancing, and even their pawns shall always be given a head start.

SCENE 17

A bell tolls as the aliʻi all walk slowly and solemnly downstage, with LILIHA and KEKŪANAŌʻA announcing the death of KAʻAHUMANU.

KEKŪANAŌʻA

Ua make o Kaʻahumanu!

LILIHA

Ua make o Kaʻahumanu!

KEKŪANAŌʻA

Ua make Kaʻahumanu!

(The aliʻi each cry their own ʻauwe ending on Kinaʻu.)

KĪNAʻU

ʻAuwē!

(KĪNAʻU sobbing)

KĪNAʻU

ʻAuwē....

(Gunshots resound as KĪNAʻU, KAUIKEAOULI, HIRAM, and several others weep.

Lei hang all around large tapestries at KAʻAHUMANU's funeral, in a chapel packed as full as can be, with many weeping on lauhala mats. KAUIKEAOULI sits in the front row of the mats with KĪNAʻU and other members of the family. HIRAM stands at the front of the church, his face still covered in tears, giving her eulogy.)

HIRAM

Shortly following the arrival of my family and I into the isles, I built a rocking chair for my wife, Sybil, a chair which many came to admire, most notably the great Queen Regent. Kaʻahumanu's request for me to build her a replica was a request I would never think of denying. 'Twas the first piece of Koa furniture that remained in her home until her very last breath. She loved that rocker, but not as much as she loved this nation. She treated her people and our people with the same maternal kindness and love she bestowed upon her own children, and that shall be never forgotten. It is my hope that her firmly planted shoes may properly be filled.

I visited her bedside on each of her final days of sickness, her strength withering with the hours that passed. "Here I am, O Jesus . . . grant me with a gracious smile." she spoke in her final moments. As she descended deep into the valley, she called to me. "Is this Bingham?" And when I confirmed, she continued, "I am going now."

The great Queen Regent Ka'ahumanu sought salvation for the people of Hawaii, and, in doing so, carved a place for herself in Heaven.

And thus, I bid her adieu, as she ascended, to go forth to her new home with Christ. The resounding bell that was tolled was slow and solemn, and with it my ear was struck as it never had been since my arrival in the Sandwich Isles.

Oh Jesus, our lord, we lay prostrate at your feet.
For there we cannot die;
Grant us thy gracious smile:
But if, for sin, we perish,
Thy law is righteous still.
We lean on thee, o lord, and hope to dwell with thee forever. Amen.

SCENE 18

KAUIKEAOULI walks outside the church after the service. He walks far enough from the crowd that he is not within earshot. Then he starts to cry. At first, it is just tears and light sobbing. Then he fully breaks down, falling onto his knees, wailing heavily. KAOMI comes to his side.

KAOMI
Kauikeaouli!

KAUIKEAOULI
My deep apologies. Likely shall the missionaries soon attempt to outlaw tears as well.

KAOMI
The Queen Regent was well aware of how full your heart was with love for her.

KAUIKEAOULI
The skies I look up to are painted in colors of doubt. My last words to her were far less than kind.

KAOMI
You mustn't continue to lash your spirit so.

(KAOMI hugs KAUIKEAOULI tightly.)

KAOMI
What is in your heart and na'au can be seen from oceans away. Struggled much have both of you to put that aloha into words, and with them you have cut each other many times.

KAUIKEAOULI
Forgive my spirits for not being instantly lifted by this speech.

KAOMI
But words are seldom the strongest manner through which aloha shines through. Kuhina Nui Ka'ahumanu so desperately desired to provide you protection that wounded you deeply. And whilst you continued to rebel against her, 'twas to protect the land and culture she loved so much. I am certain that now, with her spirit at peace, that aloha is all that remains.

SCENE 19

KĪNA'U narrates as KAUIKEAOULI and KAOMI appear in front of the palace steps to address the nation.

KĪNA'U
For the past two years, we have ushered in the time of Kaomi.

A time in which restraint ceased to exist. A time of indulgence, a time of rebellion, a time in which the clock's hands wore crooked from excessive tinkering. A time during which my brother's pure intentions of revitalizing our past outweighed his need to ensure our future.

KAUIKEAOULI

Aloha Kakou, e ka po'e Hawaii.

It is during this time of grief and recovery, that move forward as a nation we must, carrying with us our heavily weighted hearts. The passing of Queen Regent Ka'ahumanu has stung deep within each of our na'au, and it is my kuleana to continue construction of the great nation she has built. While many of you have heard rumours concerning the appointment of my new co-chief, it is my bittersweet pleasure in this trying time to officially introduce him. A man with a more visible heart than my own, an expert in the ways of healing and the ways of God.

A man whom, as the rumours may state, I love very deeply. Please welcome, with wide open arms, mō'ī Kaomi.

KAOMI

Aloha mai kākou. It is with great humility that I stand here on this still sad day.

Sure I am that many of you wonder why a poor Maui-born half-caste has been chosen to assist in the leadership of this great kingdom. I've come not to be served, but to serve, Matthew 20:28.

Outside of my ministry, I am a practitioner of the healing arts, with which I hope to aid the visceral wounds from which this nation profusely continues to bleed.

Fully capsized, our ship may appear to become fuller with ocean water with each day, sinking rapidly into the depths of the sea. Yet ferociously we shall paddle to, continue flying our sails higher than ever.

Our traditions do not conflict with Christ's teachings: Jesus is love, all love, love in all its forms—love that connects all creation.

KĪNA'U

Kauikeaouli's fixation on taking an iron hammer to everything we have built is what nearly crumbled this nation. Sin or not, my brother chose to lead a life too perilous in the national reality he so desperately attempted to flee from, in which the welcome of the days of old had long since been worn out.

The third carrier of the Kamehameha name, my brother, refused to reside here. He was of the incessant belief that within a higher, exalted reality he resided, in which one man could run the nation single-handedly, whilst his remaining hand rested gently upon the chest of another man. A reality in which this kingdom, this nation, these islands, were not held hostage.

Kyle Conner as HIRAM BINGHAM, Marie Richter as LILIHA, and Noah Nakachi as BOKI at Palikū Theatre

Jeremy Keuma as KAIHUHANUNA, Leleaʻe "Buffy" Kahalepuna-Wong as KAʻAHUMANU, and Maya Mahinalani Berengue as KĪNAʻU at Palikū Theatre

Marie Richter as LILIHA, Zaden Jay Brub as KIMO, Alaka'i Cunningham as KAPILI, Noah Nakachi as BOKI, and Jaden Manibog as ZIMO at Palikū Theatre

Corin Kumakani Medeiros as KAUIKEAOULI and Alten Keoki Ken Kiakona as KAOMI at Palikū Theatre

Jake Escoto as KEKŪANAŌʻA and Maya Mahinalani Berengue as KĪNAʻU at Palikū Theatre

Phillip Ikaika Foster as KAIKIOʻEWA and Jeremy Keuma as KAIHUHANUNA at Palikū Theatre

ACT TWO

SCENE 1

A man meets with KAOMI *in his chambers.*

MAN

I wish not for you to venture into a political disaster for my family and I. But I know not of whom else to approach.

KAOMI

With due respects to the visiting merchants, no justice is there in separating you from your ʻāina hanau, and as Saint Augustine once stated, a law that is not just is not actually a law.

*(*KAOMI *signs off on a land deed, stamping it with a royal stamp.* KAOMI *smiles at the man as he hands him the deed.)*

MAN

I am . . . overwhelmed with gratitude.

KAOMI

No thanks I am worthy of in this regard. If I may speak so boldly, some haoles have conjured fictional rights to what is yours, and an aspect of my royal duties is to correct that fiction.

MAN

Mahalo nui, mōʻī Kaomi.

KAOMI

Please. Despite this unfathomable position, I am still but a humble man of Lahaina.

MAN

Thank you again.

KAPILI

Is Your Highness prepared for the following visitor?

KAOMI

Much debate exists within the chambers regarding my true status in this kingdom.

KAPILI

That debate doesn't exist in my heart, mōʻī Kaomi.

KAOMI

While the continued churning of my insides may state otherwise, that means many worlds to me, e Kapili.

KAPILI

I shall fetch your next visitor.

(KAPILI leaves the room. He shortly returns with KAUIKEAOULI.)

KAOMI

Your Majesty.

KAUIKEAOULI

You are now moʻī as well, Kaomi, thus, quite null the formalities have become.

KAOMI

That commoner, as of yet, remains quite alive, Your Majesty. Often unsure I am of my belonging here.

KAUIKEAOULI

Perhaps it is best to perceive yourself as hanai Royalty.

KAOMI

The power to alter the world's perception belongs not in your hands. You are only king in palapala, after all.

KAUIKEAOULI

Yet it is palapala upon which this new world turns.

KAPILI

May I provide anything else to either of you aside from privacy? Would either of you care to utilize my back as a footstool, perhaps?

KAOMI

You have done plenty, e Kapili.

KAUIKEAOULI

Yes, please feel at ease to take your leave for the remainder of the day.

KAPILI

Mahalo nui loa, mōʻī Kauikeaouli and mōʻī Kaomi.

KAUIKEAOULI

It's proven more difficult to find moments alone with you than to locate Elepaio feathers.

(KAUIKEAOULI kisses KAOMI, who kisses back, then pulls away nervously.)

KAOMI

We mustn't do this in so much royal company.

KAUIKEAOULI

Have you any better suggestions, I won't hesitate in following your lead.

KAOMI
Is this house not kapu?

KAUIKEAOULI
I seem to recall some tale of the Queen Regent having the kapu system abolished.

KAOMI
You mustn't jest with me. I've no intention of degrading the royal ranks.

KAUIKEAOULI
I find that quite unfortunate.

KAOMI
I am not a man who rots the ali'i's houses from inside the walls!

KAUIKEAOULI
Many church sects appear to believe otherwise.

KAOMI
Do you believe I'm unaware of that?

(KAOMI kisses KAUIKEAOULI. They share a long kiss before a knock on the door.

KAPILI entering tentatively.)

KAPILI
E kala mai, Your Majesty, you have . . . another visitor.

SCENE 2

KAOMI starts to walk out. KAIKIO'EWA enters KAUIKEAOULI's room and passes by KAOMI, giving him a strong glare before KAOMI shuffles out.

KAUIKEAOULI

Governor Kaikioʻewa! 'Tis always a pleasure.

(KAIKIOʻEWA does honi ihu with KAUIKEAOULI begrudgingly.)

KAIKIOʻEWA

Ah yes, pleasure. The crux upon which your reign is based. And what an unfamiliar manner in which to address the man who raised you.

KAUIKEAOULI

I seem to recall you berating me previously for referring to you as "father" or "Papa." It is but care that I attempt to exercise.

KAIKIOʻEWA

Many things my youthful son appears to be exercising as of late. Care, however, does not seem to be one of them.

KAUIKEAOULI

While quite moved I am that you've sailed from Kauaʻi to visit with your precious child, quite an overflowing schedule I have, and I must be meeting with my sister shortly.

KAIKIOʻEWA

By all means, do not allow me to keep you from your important work. I merely wanted to alert you of my presence and pose a few queries.

I am simply overcome with curiosity as to how many expectations of yours are being fulfilled by your acquaintance, and his presence at your side.

KAUIKEAOULI

I do not find comfort in discussing the fulfillment of my expectations with you, father. Such matters are quite personal.

KAIKIOʻEWA

Few qualms you seem to have with the blurring of lines between the personal and the political thus far. Few qualms you seem to have with exclaiming the personal for the populace of each island to hear. I see not why a vow of silence you must suddenly take on. . . .

KAUIKEAOULI
I merely find difficulty trusting in the ability of your ears to receive my words without twisting them into a rope to be fastened upon my neck.

KAIKIOʻEWA
'Tis quite appalling that you would imagine your neck to be the area of fascination.

KAUIKEAOULI
While highly do I regard your words, I believe it best for the both of us that you leave my chambers, before I peer too deeply into their potential interpretations.

KAIKIOʻEWA
Very well, my son. I shall be seeing you shortly.

(KAIKIOʻEWA exits. Several members of the hulumanu, including KAPILI and BOKI enter, singing, dancing, drunken and full of joy.)

KAPILI
It is natural to behave in a loving manner!
It is the dawn of a new day!

SCENE 3

KAUIKEAOULI walks into KĪNAʻU's chambers.

KAUIKEAOULI
Aloha mai, Kīnaʻu. To what do I owe this particular summons?

KĪNAʻU
Oh what indeed, brother.

KAUIKEAOULI

Even in your fantasy realm in which I would for a second consider removing Kaomi from his post, it is far too late to do so.

KĪNAʻU

The ʻiwi of our Kuhina nui churn in Pohukaina at your stubbornness.

KAUIKEAOULI

'Tis far too early for me to receive this barrage of fire.

KĪNAʻU

Much support and understanding I am attempting to show, but other aliʻi do not share my level of patience. Especially those who view you as a barrier in the path to Christ.

KAUIKEAOULI

Is it the Kauaʻi governor of whom you speak? Is he not the most accepting father a son could ever wish for?

KĪNAʻU

Then what of the ardent spirit distilleries for which you repealed laws to allow them to conduct business? What of the numerous land grants handed out to commoners by your co-chief? I am aware of the righteousness you believe you are exhibiting, but you appear to forget the unbreakable bricks the merchants and missionaries have used to assist in our building of this palace!

KAUIKEAOULI

As usual, in your arguments I see much contradiction. Many of those bricks have been placed by merchants I am returning business to, such as those involved in the sale of liquor.

KĪNAʻU

I believe within your best interest it would be not to attempt the splitting of hairs. It is not for you to choose which foreign influences to accommodate, and which to greatly displease.

KAUIKEAOULI

On the contrary, I believe that as king, it is my choice alone. Choice being a luxury that I shall remind you I was seldomly offered previously.

KĪNAʻU

Choice has never been afforded to a single one of us!

KAUIKEAOULI

I find myself curious as to Kuhina Nui Kaʻahumanu's abolishing of the kapu system only for our tongues to remain beneath an ever-growing pile of man-made stones.

KĪNAʻU

You dare speak the Queen Regent's name so disrespectfully here?! Tirelessly she worked to enact laws that you continue to shatter with your disregard. Perhaps hers were too lenient, and new laws must be set forth.

KAUIKEAOULI

Perhaps you are correct. Perhaps there exist too many laws which allow others to challenge the king's authority so blithely. Perhaps a law must be decreed which would prevent such perpetual insolence.

KĪNAʻU

Even you would not dare.

KAUIKEAOULI

You ought to know how fatal of a flaw underestimating me can be.

(KAUIKEAOULI storms out of KĪNAʻU's chambers.)

SCENE 4

Two of the royal guard walk by, solemnly carrying a funeral bier. On it, a small body is draped in a sheet. Other members of the hulumanu walk with them in a funeral procession. KAUIKEAOULI *watches with his arm around* KAOMI, *smirking and stifling laughter.*

LILIHA

Romans 8:38–39: "For I am convinced that neither death nor life, neither angels nor demons, neither the present nor the future, nor any powers, neither height nor depth, nor anything else in all creation, will be able to separate us from the love of God that is in Christ Jesus our Lord."

KAPILI

God rest his baboon soul.

(The funeral procession exits past HIRAM *and* KAIKIOʻEWA, *who have been watching the proceedings with burning rage and disgust.)*

HIRAM

Is it pride that you look upon your adopted prodigal son on this day?

KAIKIOʻEWA

I no longer know what it is I feel when I look upon him. Staunchly do I applaud the unwithering torch of burning love he carries for this culture of ours... but this hulumanu... worry fills me that birds of a feather shall flock to extinction.

HIRAM

Well, worry not, as he has the former minister on whom I imparted much knowledge at his side. I am certain that will ensure much smooth sailing.

KAIKIOʻEWA

That Kaomi I shall never understand. What drives a man so far opposite The Lord? I too carry deep love for our traditions, but so lost I was before receiving the blessing of Scripture. How one can abandon his blessed post so readily to jump aboard the helm of this leaking ship shall forever exceed my perception. Would that he were still stationed behind Lahaina stained glass....

HIRAM

One's emotions can drive one to do many unspeakable things, such as transforming the loud mourning of a baboon into sardonic mockery of the great Lord. Two men who are so strongly pulled by lust may not be fit to stabilize this nation.

KAIKIOʻEWA

Were it simply lust pulling them, I think not that this predicament would have escalated with such severity. I cannot see their love as something so simply brash, for I was similarly loved by Kamehameha the Great. No hypocrisy I would like to show. True aloha exists between them, but it is infused with the spirit of kuʻe.

HIRAM

Resistance, while admirable, does not create a proper king. Moreover, it creates buffoons who stage elaborate theatrical pieces posing as funeral services for their ludicrous pets.

KAIKIOʻEWA

Perhaps merely the stubbornness of youth this is. Perhaps we are merely experiencing the consequences of my young hanai son being placed in the throne so prematurely. Perhaps this is yet another phase of the moon.

HIRAM

But do you think it wise to live in a sea of "perhaps"?

(HIRAM and KAIKIOʻEWA exit. KAUIKEAOULI squeezes KAOMI tighter and smiles.)

KAUIKEAOULI

Is royalty not grand?

KAOMI

I must with great respect inquire as to what it is I have heard of you declaring a tyranny.

KAUIKEAOULI

What you have heard is a radical interpretation of my kingly duties.

KAOMI

And should I presume those kingly duties now involve usurping the power of every other member of the court?

KAUIKEAOULI

Was it not you that stated that I am "king only in palapala"? Perhaps it's time to fix that.

KAOMI

It seems we have yet another instance we have reached in which you have twisted the intent of my words like hau vines.

KAUIKEAOULI

Is the hau vine not where you gathered this news?

KAOMI

I just worry that we'll become further entangled and unable to exit the forest.

KAUIKEAOULI

Magnificent. It's my hope for that forest to reach as vastly as possible.

SCENE 5

KAIKIOʻEWA and KĪNAʻU meet in her chambers.

KAIKIOʻEWA

No substance I thought there was to that threat?! Such audacity would far exceed even his reach!

KĪNAʻU

I garner no excitement from this either. The unavoidable truth is that my brother has decreed a law which prevents any of us from setting forth our own without his approval.

KAIKIOʻEWA

Is receiving a mutiny a strong desire of his?!

KĪNAʻU

Calm yourself, Governor Kaikioʻewa. No good will come of shouting improper words.

KAIKIOʻEWA

Then I ask, what good shall come of shouting nothing?

KĪNAʻU

Since his seem to be quite busy recklessly flailing, perhaps it is time that within our own hands we take this kingdom.

KAIKIOʻEWA

And how might we conduct such a task?

KĪNAʻU

An excellent query. To answer it, I believe a plan we should begin to concoct.

KAIKIOʻEWA

A plan to remove that Kaomi from his side?! This is something I could arrange quite imminently.

KĪNAʻU

I fail to see how further recklessness would improve the situation at hand. And it was my impression that despite the ensuing chaos, your feelings regarding their relationship were still in much conflict.

KAIKIOʻEWA

Rage is beginning to become quite victorious in that conflict.

KĪNAʻU
How wondrous.

SCENE 6

KAOMI sits with BOKI and LILIHA at a dining table in front of their home, eating chocolates.

BOKI
Yes, Kaomi, when are these missionaries leaving is my question as well. Please Kaomi, feel free to indulge in some chocolate treats.

KAOMI
While much appreciation do I feel for the offer, I believe further indulgence may not be the most proper avenue for me at this time.

LILIHA
Come now, Kaomi. These imports are some of the few benefits of the invasive merchants. Enjoyment of this ever-so-sweet silver lining is paramount to motivate one's continued survival.

BOKI
My kolohe rascal wife is quite right.

(KAIKIOʻEWA and KAIHUHANUNA walk over, to the surprise of the others.)

LILIHA
Ah, aloha mai, Governor Kaikioʻewa. Why did none inform me you had not yet returned to Kauai? While you remain here, would you like to join us for foreign delights?

KAIKIOʻEWA
It is not within my custom to break bread with half-castes who should not have been invited into the throneroom.

BOKI

I assure you, Governor, there is no bread, so I believe your customs will remain intact.

KAIKIOʻEWA

Much unlike this kingdom.

LILIHA

Very puzzling do I find it that the Governor of Kauaʻi sailed all this way simply to mount a display of petty insecurity.

BOKI

It seems you've some amnesia regarding my wife's title of Governor, and the fact that you are currently in her jurisdiction.

KAIHUHANUNA

Ah, is that the scent of chocolate? Oh please, Governor Kaikioʻewa, could we stay only for a moment? Chocolate fills me with delight, and seldom do we receive shipments in Kauaʻi.

KAIKIOʻEWA

If you continue providing a divided front, perhaps I shall leave you here to gorge on all the chocolate you please.

LILIHA

If this gathering is truly so far beneath you, Kaihuhanuna may take some chocolate with him.

KAIHUHANUNA

Oh, would you really? God bless, Governor Liliha and Boki. My heart, which shall be beating much faster in a moment, is filled with gratitude.

KAIKIOʻEWA

Procure your own servants, Liliha. Do not attempt to buy off mine so cheaply!

BOKI

All right, quite a foul mood you appear to be in, and so perhaps it is best we for now bid you adieu, so as to prevent any further casualties.

KAIKIOʻEWA

I shan't participate in your idle games and leisurely banter whilst my nation is sunk into the depths by the hedonist that seems to be becoming of my progeny! So you are quite correct. This gathering *is* beneath me.

KAOMI

That's quite enough!

KAOMI

I must humbly and with great respect state that if it is your wish to insult my heritage and way of life... if it is your wish to pull my seat from this table so quickly so that I might break my back... those are wishes I shan't deny you.

But if it is your wish to degenerate our king... our fearless leader, who would to the bottom of the ocean dive down for his people... that is a wish I shall never be capable of granting!

(After staring at KAOMI for a few moments, KAIKIOʻEWA, without warning, punches him square in the jaw, knocking him at the feet of LILIHA and BOKI, who immediately pick him up and check that he's all right.)

KAIKIOʻEWA

Come now, Kaihuhanuna. We must depart these grounds, for they appear to be deeply submerged in polluted waters.

SCENE 7

Two distillery workers, KALEO and KŪLANI, sit on the floor of a distillery, singing and throwing dice as KAIKIOʻEWA and KAIHUHANUNA enter.

KAIKIOʻEWA

Happy is the land whose king is a noble leader and whose leaders feast at the proper time to gain strength for their work, not to get drunk. Ecclesiastes 10:17.

KALEO

Mōʻī Kaomi's distillery this is. If in need of rum and relaxation you are, we can be of assistance.

KŪLANI

A generous day of benevolent leisure Mōʻī Kaomi has given the other workers—our apologies please accept, for we are the only ones here to see to your needs, chief Kaīkiʻoewa.

KAIKIOʻEWA

No need for your liquor have I or anyone!

(KAIHUHANUNA punches KALEO and before KŪLANI can react, kicks him in the knee, knocking them both down.)

KAIHUHANUNA

Wake up, you drunkards, and weep! Wail, all you drinkers of wine.

Look not thou upon the wine when it is red, when it giveth his colour in the cup, when it moveth itself aright. At the last it biteth like a serpent, and stingeth like an adder. Thine eyes shall behold strange women, and thine heart shall utter perverse things.

(KAIKIOʻEWA carries with him a large bayonet, which he uses to hit the barrels, which shoot out liquor.)

KAIKIOʻEWA

For you have spent enough time in the past doing what pagans choose to do—living in debauchery, lust, drunkenness, orgies, carousing and detestable idolatry. They are surprised that you do not join them in their reckless, wild living, and they heap abuse on you.

SCENE 8

Late at night, KAUIKEAOULI *is awakened in his bed by* KAPILI.

KAPILI
My deepest mihi, Your Highness, but Governor Liliha is here to see you.

KAUIKEAOULI
Can it not wait till morning?

KAPILI
If it is Your Majesty's wish for me to be beaten like kapa, then by all means, let me be the one to turn her away.

*(*KAUIKEAOULI *sighs and motions for them to be sent in.* BOKI *and* LILIHA *enter.* LILIHA *holds a large gin bottle she takes periodic swigs from.)*

LILIHA
That sister of yours is equipped with some gargantuan olos.

KAUIKEAOULI
From whence has the volume of my sister's olos ranked such importance?

LILIHA
Perhaps since two of our distilleries have been attacked.

KAUIKEAOULI
Forgive my confusion in regards to what you mean by "attacked."

LILIHA
Decimated tanks are gushing liquor like freshwater springs . . . workers bruised and bloodied . . . it is quite the unnatural disaster.

KAUIKEAOULI
And you believe Kīnaʻu is to blame for this?

LILIHA
One of those distilleries belongs to Kaomi.

(KAUIKEAOULI stands up, angrily.)

KAUIKEAOULI
I shall speak to Kīnaʻu.

LILIHA
I'm glad that your interest has finally been piqued.

KAUIKEAOULI
Well, if implications you'd like to make regarding my priority of interests, perhaps Kīnaʻu and yourself may see eye to eye, rather than an eye for an eye.

LILIHA
I ask that you spare me of your attitude, O Great King. Forget not who has provided endless kako'o and support throughout the journey we politely call a reign.

KAUIKEAOULI
Perhaps you should not have helped keep me in this throne, had you no intention of respecting my place in it.

LILIHA
How is such audacity provided to you? Do you think lightly of my own duties to this nation, both as Governor and Kuhina Nui?! Do you not think this attack makes those duties endlessly difficult?

KAUIKEAOULI
My apologies, Governor Liliha. The distress plaguing my naʻau has led to my mouth uttering falsities.

LILIHA
Well, it would be best if you attempt to revitalize that naʻau, for its guidance is needed more than ever.

KAUIKEAOULI
Perhaps my guidance is what leads us astray.

SCENE 9

KĪNA'U strolls through the palace grounds. KAUIKEAOULI walks briskly and angrily toward her.

KĪNA'U
I believe your royal 'aikāne may be a more suitable shoulder to weep on.

KAUIKEAOULI
Oh thank heavens. You acknowledge our relationship at last. Contentedly Kaomi and I might perish yet.

KĪNA'U
I think it wise you show gratitude for the fact that you have yet to, as I exhaustively have worked to prevent that.

KAUIKEAOULI
Have you any clue the assistance those distilleries have provided our economy?

KĪNA'U
We have already spoken of this. Brandishing your disregard for every law that you did not personally write is hardly economical.

KAUIKEAOULI
You are not exactly following each letter either.

KĪNA'U
Did you consider that I simply tire of white missionaries calling us a kingdom of satanic savages?! What on Earth or any other planet would you have me do?

KAUIKEAOULI

Stand beside me, perhaps. Stand beside our people, whose love is shackled by your friends, the missionaries. Stand by our culture, as we raise it from its mass grave.

KĪNAʻU

Corpses need not be revitalized!

KAUIKEAOULI

Is that the manner in which you view Kaomi and I? As corpses?

KĪNAʻU

In my utter failure to protect either of you from such a fate, I feel that could soon be what becomes of the both of you.

SCENE 10

KAOMI sits in front of an ʻahu in his backyard, praying.

KAOMI

E nā akua . . . *and* ke akua . . . I humbly beg you to tell me why it is that I remain here. . . .

While forever grateful I am for this unorthodox opportunity to serve my kingdom . . . and to be granted the power and privilege to give back to our people in need . . . many questions I have had in regards to a few of my latest blessings . . . for which I once again beg your forgiveness.

I feel as though I have been handed one of the reins to a kingdom that is not mine to handle. . . .

But no matter how out of place they feel in my grasp . . . they won't vanish from betwixt my fingertips . . . and to release and discard them would be a greater, more wasteful sin. . . .

On the subject of sin . . . the pleasures I find with my king . . . I know cannot be sin, incredibly righteous they feel . . . not only the love we share, but the manner in which we are able to give this nation back to the people it continues to be commandeered from. I thank you for these gifts of pleasure.

(KAIHUHANUNA and KAIKIOʻEWA, along with a group of soldiers, walk into the yard, weapons out. KAIKIOʻEWA carries a musket with him. KAOMI does not see them approaching from behind him.)

KAIHUHANUNA

Are you certain this is ethical, Governor Kaikioʻewa?

KAUIKEAOULI

We are preventing a half-caste from continuing to rot this kingdom from the inside out . . . nothing more ethical am I able to imagine.

KAIHUHANUNA

My apologies for questioning you, sir. I am merely hard of thinking.

KAOMI

I have heard the devil's speech patterns . . . I have heard him raise his voice . . . heard him stutter between whispers . . . I have heard the calm in his voice when he tells me to follow him . . . and he sounds nothing like Kauikeaouli . . . .

He sounds nothing like . . . my love. . . .
He sounds nothing like . . . my people . . .
and he sounds nothing like . . . you. . . .

(KAIKIOʻEWA points his musket at KAOMI.)

KAIKIOʻEWA

On the sound of the devil's voice you shall gain a much stronger grasp . . . once we have returned you to him.

(KAOMI turns around, shocked, afraid, but accepting the situation with tragic grace.)

KAOMI

If death be my prophecy, death it shall be.

(KAIHUHANUNA grabs KAOMI and strikes him a couple of times before handing him off to KAIKIOʻEWA, who punches KAOMI repeatedly as KAIHUHANUNA wraps KAOMI with rope. KAIKIOʻEWA motions for KAIHUHANUNA to hit KAOMI too, which he's very hesitant to do, but does once threatened. Running over after being alerted of commotion by one of her messengers, KĪNAʻU walks into the yard and sees, horrified.)

KĪNAʻU

What in the name of the Lord you claim to serve do you fools think you're doing?!

KAIKIOʻEWA A

I believe the answer to be quite self-evident.

KĪNAʻU

Have you any clue the number of heads Kauikeaouli will have roll for this?! Yours will be the first tumbling down the koʻolau ridges, and I shan't be there to catch it!

I am unable to condone such behavior. You've outdone even the king himself with your carelessness.

KAIKIOʻEWA

Whatever have we spoken of in countless meetings??

KĪNAʻU

I shall not be held to blame for your sore misinterpretation of my concerns!

KAIKIOʻEWA

This defected half-caste's lover is neither your king nor mine, an understanding I believed we shared.

KĪNA'U

And I believed we shared an understanding that such a loosely woven plan would be far out of the question!

(KAPILI, on royal guard duty, overhears this right outside their quarters, and immediately runs to KAUIKEAOULI's quarters. KAUIKEAOULI wakes up out of bed when KAPILI comes to his bedside.)

KAPILI

Your Majesty! Kaikio'ewa is attempting to end Kaomi's life and I had no part in it!

(KAUIKEAOULI storms in, fully clad in silk sleepwear, immediately pushing KAIHUHANUNA away from KAOMI into the wall, and starts untying KAOMI's binds. As soon as he fully unties KAOMI, KAUIKEAOULI lunges at KAIKIO'EWA, grappling with him on the ground.)

KAIKIO'EWA

Here returns my prodigal son! You are not the ruler of this kingdom if you continue to indulge yourself in these evil ways!

(Without responding, KAUIKEAOULI continues grappling with KAIKIO'EWA. KAUIKEAOULI gets on top, holding his hand over KAIKIO'EWA's neck, then gets up at the last second, leaving him on the ground. He helps KAOMI up, and walks him out. Before walking out, KAUIKEAOULI looks at KAIKIO'EWA sadly.)

SCENE 11

The sounds of water fill the air as KAUIKEAOULI tenderly caresses KAOMI's hair while he sleeps. KAOMI wakes up.

KAOMI

My love . . . what has happened—where are w—

KAUIKEAOULI

Shhhh. Your injuries. From speaking much you must refrain.

(KAUIKEAOULI puts a wet hand towel on KAOMI's forehead.)

KAUIKEAOULI

I am . . . returning you home.

KAOMI

But your royal duties—

KAUIKEAOULI

—can be held off. Besides, it has been made clearer than our cleanest waterfalls that the nation shan't weather the storm properly with me at the helm.

KAOMI

Nonsense, this nation has never had a greater captain!

KAUIKEAOULI

Worry not, Kaomi. I don't intend to jump ship. I merely believe it healthy to spend some time on land . . . to be with the man I love the most.

KAOMI

I'm deeply sorry, my king. By falling overboard, I have pulled you further and further from your throne, into the deep ocean.

KAUIKEAOULI

That throne provided no proper back support anyhow. And it was I who was to blame for your drowning.

KAOMI

On this we will never agree... but I will beg you a thousand times to forgive me... for what my love has cost you.

KAUIKEAOULI

I am the one in dire need of forgiveness, Kaomi. My embrace has dragged you to the depths of the place written in those scriptures I have refused to brand on my skin. And here you are, burning every day for my selfishness. For my need to have you by my side even when that side is engulfed in flame.

KAOMI

Never, Your Majesty, would I trade none of it for the world. Even a world better than this one.

(KAUIKEAOULI starts crying, and just holds KAOMI for a long time.)

KAUIKEAOULI

I wish not to discuss details surrounding the light fading in Kaomi's eyes, but rather the storm I so recklessly steered him into....

Had he not joined me on this vessel... a chance he may have had to sail beneath skies filled with stars to map the path ahead. This captain instead sailed under thunderous clouds through which not a star could be seen. Clear those skies have become in the eye I've reached much too late, and far overboard the man I love has fallen with no rope left to pull him upwards. No breath do I have left to push back into his saltwater-filled lungs, nor to breathe color into this nation.

The moment the man I love died, so did the torch of ku'e within me... the flame submerged in an instant... as if never before had it been lit...

What reason is left to continue battle? All that seemed to come of it was red stains embedded into my fingertips I have no intention of scrubbing away... for they are all that is left of the beautiful healer who hailed from Lahaina into the center of my heart... this way, it is as if our fingers are forever interlocked....

For vengeance they believe they have opened deep within my na'au... but... the fight in me has been extinguished....

SCENE 12

A loudly murmuring crowd fills the palace grounds, waiting for the king's address. KAUIKEAOULI *comes down the palace steps slowly, devoid of the mischievous sparkle in his usually slightly crinkled eyes. He stares straight ahead, almost as if in a trance, as he greets the audience.*

KAUIKEAOULI

Aloha mai, people of Oahu. I would like to apologize greatly for my neglect of this nation. I have not been the leader Hawaii has been in desperate need of and... my reckless actions have endangered the people and the kingdom I love so dearly. Further bloodshed is not my desire.

KAUIKEAOULI

My desire now is to honor the structure of this palace we have built, and rebuild it, brick by brick.

A wise and great man once told me that much akin to the sails of a ship in the turbulent wind, healing is a process that seldom charges straightforwardly. It is with an ebb and flow in which we must learn to rock and sway does it move.

And amidst this perilous voyage, we call upon Ke Akua, and our ancestors who look down upon us from his side, and our long lost loved ones to show us the way, as they have always done, and always will.

KAUIKEAOULI

And one day, I hope to reach the shores... Kaomi has been carried off to.

AFTERWORD

Hawaiian historian Kanalu Young described the past as "a pūʻolo (leaf-wrapped bundle) of bygone eras, the endpoint of which at any given moment is never reached.... The pūʻolo, in its hypothetical entirety, happened once, although historical studies, like polyps on a reef, increase the size of the overall body of knowledge about the ʻŌiwi past."

Hawaiʻi's dominant real estate and tourism industry is deeply conditioned by historical narratives shaped in the plantation era. The way history is remembered—and what is emphasized or omitted—plays a crucial role in shaping present-day perceptions. For too long, Hawaiʻi history has been dominated by a narrative placing the real estate and tourism industry as a logical evolution from the plantation era. This plantation-origin story minimizes and omits complex, contradictory events of especially Hawaiian political and social development, in order to reinforce a sense of the inevitability of today's tourism-driven economy as the only viable path forward.

Hawaiian scholar Lilikalā Kameʻeleihiwa cautioned, "Hawaiian society [will n]ever be pono again until we Hawaiian people come to know our history intimately and until we can understand the challenges faced by the Mōʻī Kauikeaouli who made the 1848 Mahele.... The most important question of Kauikeaouli's life was how he would become a pono Mōʻī."

Kameʻeleihiwa described the historical events that shaped Kauikeaouli's reign as part of the traditional struggle of a new paramount ruler to establish pono rule following Kaʻahumanu's death. This struggle is often framed as a clash between a traditional Hawaiian lifestyle, embodied by the Makahonu of Liholiho, and the new Christian kapu introduced by Hiram Bingham and the American missionaries.

Even the simplified Christian-versus-non-Christian binary often used to describe the ideological struggles of this period is complicated by Kaomi's time—a young, Maui-born, hapa Hawaiian-Boraboran Christian preacher who became the intimate partner of Kauikeaouli. A more accurate framing may be a struggle between American Calvinism and Hawaiian worldviews—including those that integrated useful elements of Christian thought.

Telling Kaomi's story provides an opportunity to reconsider the dominant historical narratives that frame Hawaiʻi's transformation into a U.S. state shaped by tourism and real estate development. It is also a story about traditional Hawaiian sexual affinities and relationships between intimate and social lives. Kaomi was not only a sexual partner, but a leader with iconoclastic values that he mobilized in political spheres. As Hawaiian historian Adam Manalo-Camp wrote, Kaomi represents "not just as a 'queer icon,' but . . . an early Polynesian leader of resistance to assimilation."

Lance D. Collins
Producer of the World Premiere

Further Reading

Kameʻeleihiwa, Lilikalā. *Native Land and Foreign Desires: Pehea Lā E Pono Ai?* Bishop Museum Press, 1992.

Manalo-Camp, Adam Keawe. "Ka Wā Iā Kaomi: The Time of Kaomi." In *Historical Investigations in West Maui*, edited by Lance D. Collins and Bianca K. Isaki. North Beach-West Maui Benefit Fund, 2024.

Teves, Stephanie Nohelani. *The Mahele of Our Bodies: Nā Moʻolelo Kūpuna Māhū/ LGBTQ*. University of Hawaiʻi Press, 2025.

Young, Kanalu G. Terry. *Rethinking the Native Hawaiian Past*. Routledge, 1998.

About the Author

Noalani Helelā is a severely neurodivergent Hapa Hawaiian-Japanese-Chinese artist whose work includes filmmaking, playwriting, music, and poetry. After competing in several national poetry slams, she made her playwriting debut with Demigods Anonymous at Kumu Kahua Theatre in 2018, which saw a second staging at Palikū Theatre in fall 2022. She also wrote, directed, and starred in the short film *Yellow Fever Aftermath* in 2020 for Windward Academy of Creative Media.